Arthur Machen (1863–1947) was a Welsh author best known for his works of supernatural fiction, such as *The Great God Pan* (1894), *The Three Impostors* (1895), and *The White People* (1904). He is widely considered to be one of the greatest writers of horror fiction in the English language.

ARTHUR MACHEN

1

THEY were talking about old days and old ways and all the changes that have come on London in the last weary years; a little party of three of them, gathered for a rare meeting in Perrott's rooms.

One man, the youngest of the three, a lad of fifty-five or so, had begun to say:

"I know every inch of that neighbourhood, and I tell you there's no such place."

His name was Harliss; and he was supposed to have something to do with chemicals and carboys and crystals.

They had been recalling many London vicissitudes, these three; and it must be noted that the boy of the party, Harliss, could remember very well the Strand as it used to be, before they spoilt it all. Indeed, if he could not have gone as far back as the years of those doings, it is doubtful whether Perrott would have let him into the meeting in Mitre Place, an alley which was an entrance of the inn by day, but was blind after nine o'clock at night, when the iron gates were shut, and the pavement grew silent. The rooms were on the second floor, and from the front windows could be seen the elms in the inn garden, where the rooks used to build before the war. Within, the large, low room was softly, deeply carpeted from wall to wall; the winter night, with a bitter dry wind rising, and moaning even in the heart of London, was shut out by thick crimson curtains, and the three then sat about a blazing fire in an old fireplace, a fireplace that stood high from the hearth, with hobs on each side of it, and a big kettle beginning to murmur on one of them. The armchairs on which the three sat were of the sort that Mr. Pickwick sits on for ever in his frontispiece. The round table of dark mahogany stood on one leg, very deeply and profusely carved, and Perrott said it was a George IV table, though the third friend, Arnold, held that William IV, or even very early Victoria, would have been nearer the mark. On the dark red wall-paper there were eighteenth-century engravings of Durham Cathedral and Peterborough Cathedral, which showed that, in spite of Horace Walpole and his friend Mr. Gray, the eighteenth century couldn't draw a Gothic building when its towers and traceries were before its eyes: "because they couldn't see it," Arnold had insisted, late one night, when the gliding signs were far on in their course, and the punch in the jar had begun to thicken a little on its spices. There were other engravings of a later date about the walls, things of the thirties and forties by forgotten artists, known well enough in their day; landscapes of the Valley of the Usk, and the Holy Mountain, and Llanthony: all with a certain enchantment and vision about them, as if their domed hills and solemn woods were more of grace than of nature. Over the hearth was *Bolton Abbey in the Olden Time*.

Perrott would apologize for it.

"I know," he would say. "I know all about it. It is a pig, and a goat, and a dog, and a damned nonsense"—he was quoting a Welsh story—"but it used to hang over the fire in the dining-room at home. And I often wish I had brought along *Te Deum Laudamus* as well."

"What's that?" Harliss asked.

"Ah, you're too young to have lived with it. It depicts three choir-boys in surplices; one singing for his life, and the other two looking about them—just like choir-boys. And we were always told that the busy boy was hanged at last. The companion picture showed three charity girls, also singing. This was called *Te Dominum Confitemur.* I never heard their story."

"I know." Harliss brightened. "I came upon them both in lodgings near the station at Brighton, in Mafeking year. And, a year or two later, I saw *Sherry, Sir* in an hotel at Tenby."

"The finest wax fruit I ever saw," Arnold joined in, "was in a window in the King's Cross Road."

So they would maunder along, about the old-fashioned rather than the old. And so on this winter night of the cold wind they lingered about the London streets of forty, forty-five, fifty-five years ago.

One of them dilated on Bloomsbury, in the days when the bars were up, and the Duke's porters had boxes beside the gates, and all was peace, not to say profound dullness, within those solemn boundaries. Here was the high vaulted church of a strange sect, where, they said, while the smoke of incense fumed about a solemn rite, a wailing voice would suddenly rise up with the sound of an incantation in magic. Here, another church, where Christina Rossetti bowed her head; all about, dim squares where no one walked, and the leaves of the trees were dark with smoke and soot.

"I remember one spring," said Arnold, "when they were the brightest green I ever saw. In Bloomsbury Square. Long ago."

"That wonderful little lion stood on the iron posts in the pavement in front of the British Museum," Perrott put in. "I believe they have kept a few and hidden them in museums. That's one of the reasons why the streets grow duller and duller. If there is anything curious, anything beautiful in a street, they take it away and stick it in a museum. I wonder what has become of that odd little figure, I think it was in a cocked hat, that stood by the bar-parlour door in the courtyard of the bell in Holborn."

They worked their way down by Fetter Lane, and lamented Dryden's house—"I think it was in 87 that they pulled it down"—and lingered on the site of Clifford's Inn—"you could walk into the seventeenth century"—and so at last into the Strand.

"Someone said it was the finest street in Europe."

"Yes, no doubt—in a sense. Not at all in the obvious sense; it wasn't *belle architecture de ville*. It was of all ages and all sizes and heights and styles: a unique enchantment of a street; an incantation, full of words that meant nothing to the uninitiated."

A sort of Litany followed.

"The Shop of the Pale Puddings, where little David Copperfield might have bought his dinner."

"That was close to Bookseller's Row—sixteenth-century houses."

"And 'Chocolate as in Spain'; opposite Charing Cross."

"The *Globe* office, where one sent one's early turnovers."

"The narrow alleys with steps going down to the river."

"The smell of making soap from the scent shop."

"Nutt's bookshop, near the Welsh mutton butcher's, where the street was narrow."

"The *Family Herald* office; with a picture in the window of an early type-setting machine, showing the operator working a contraption with long arms, that hovered over the case."

"And Garden House in the middle of a lawn, in Clement's Inn."

"And the flicker of those old yellow gas-lamps, when the wind blew up the street, and the people were packing into that passage that led to the Lyceum pit."

One of them, his ear caught by a phrase that another had used, began to murmur verses from "Oh, plump head waiter at the Cock."

"What chops they were!" sighed Perrott. And he began to make the punch, grating first of all the lumps of sugar against the lemons; drawing forth thereby the delicate, aromatic oils from the rind of the Mediterranean fruit. Matters were brought forth from cupboards at the dark end of the room: rum from the Jamaica Coffee House in the City, spices in blue china boxes, one or two old bottles containing secret essences. The kettle boiled, the ingredients were dusted in and poured into the red-brown jar, which was then muffled and set to digest on the hearth, in the heat of the fire.

"*Misce, fiat mistura*," said Harliss.

"Very well," answered Arnold. "But remember that all the true matters of the work are invisible."

Nobody minded him or his alchemy; and after a due interval, the glasses were held over the fragrant steam of the jar, and then filled. The three sat round the fire, drinking and sipping with grateful hearts.

2

L ET it be noted that the glasses in question held no great quantity of the hot liquor. Indeed, they were what used to be called rummers; round, and of a bloated aspect, but of comparatively small capacity. Therefore, nothing injurious to the clearness of those old heads is to be inferred, when it is said that between the third and fourth filling, the talk drew away from central London and the lost, beloved Strand and began to go farther afield, into stranger, less-known territories. Perrott began it, by tracing a curious passage he had once made northward, dodging by the Globe and the Olympic theatres into the dark labyrinth of Clare Market, under arches and by alleys, till he came into Great Queen Street, near the Freemason's Tavern and Inigo Jones's red pilasters. Another took up the tale, and drifting into Holborn by

15

Whetstone's Park, and going astray a little to visit Kingsgate Street—"just like Phiz's plate: mean, low, deplorable; but I wish they hadn't pulled it down"—finally reached Theobald's Road. There, they delayed a little, to consider curiously decorated leaden water-cisterns that were once to be seen in the areas of a few of the older houses, and also to speculate on the legend that an ancient galleried inn, now used as a warehouse, had survived till quite lately at the back of Tibbles Road—for so they called it. And thence, northward and eastward, up the Gray's Inn Road, crossing the King's Cross Road, and going up the hill.

"And here," said Arnold, "we begin to touch on the conjectured. We have left the known world behind us."

Indeed, it was he who now had the party in charge.

"Do you know," said Perrott, "that sounds awful rot, but it's true; at least so far as I am concerned. I don't think I ever went beyond Holborn Town Hall, as it used to be—I mean walking. Of course, I've driven in a hansom to King's Cross Railway Station, and I went once or twice to the Military Tournament, when it was at the Agricultural Hall, in Islington; but I don't remember how I got there."

Harliss said he had been brought up in North London, but much farther north—Stoke Newington way.

"I once knew a man," said Perrott, "who knew all about Stoke Newington; at least he ought to have known about it. He was a Poe enthusiast, and he wanted to find out whether the school where Poe boarded when he was a little boy was still standing. He went again and again; and the odd thing is that, in spite of his interest in the matter, he didn't seem to know whether the school was still there, or whether he had seen it. He spoke of certain survivals of the Stoke Newington that Poe indicates in a phrase or two in 'William Wilson': the dreamy village, the misty trees, the old rambling red-brick houses, standing in their gardens, with high walls all about them. But though he declared that he had gone so far as to interview the vicar, and could describe the old church with the dormer windows, he could never make up his mind whether he had seen Poe's school."

"I never heard of it when I lived there," said Harliss. "But I came of business stock. We didn't gossip much about authors. I have a vague sort of notion that I once heard somebody speak of Poe as a notorious drunkard—and that's about all I ever heard of him till a good deal later."

"It is queer, but it's true," Arnold broke in, "that there's a general tendency to seize on the accidental, and ignore the essential. You may be vague enough about the treble works, the vast designs of the laboured rampart lines; but at least you knew that the Duke of Wellington had a very big nose. I remember it on the tins of knife polish."

"But that fellow I was speaking of," said Perrott, going back to his topic, "I couldn't make him out. I put it to him; 'Surely you know one way or the other: this old school is still standing—or was still standing—or not: you either saw it or you didn't: there can't be any doubt about the matter.' But we couldn't get to negative or positive. He confessed that it was strange; 'But upon my word I don't know. I went once, I think, about '95, and then, again, in '99—that was the time I called on the vicar; and I have never been since.' He talked like a man who had gone into a mist, and could not speak with any certainty of the shapes he had seen in it.

"And that reminds me. Long after my talk with Hare—that was the man who was interested in Poe—a distant cousin of mine from the country came up to town to see about the affairs of an old aunt of his who had lived all her life somewhere Stoke Newington way, and had just died.

He came in here one evening to look me up—we had not met for many years—and he was saying, truly enough, I am sure, how little the average Londoner knew of London, when you once took him off his beaten track. 'For example,' he said to me, 'have you ever been in Stoke Newington?' I confessed that I hadn't, that I had never had any reason to go there. 'Exactly; and I don't suppose you've ever even heard of Canon's Park?' I confessed ignorance again. He said it was an extraordinary thing that such a beautiful place as this, within four or five miles of the centre of London, seemed absolutely unknown and unheard of by nine Londoners out of ten."

"I know every inch of that neighbourhood," broke in Harliss. "I was born there and lived there till I was sixteen. There's no such place anywhere near Stoke Newington."

"But, look here, Harliss," said Arnold. "I don't know that you're really an authority."

"Not an authority on a place I knew backwards for sixteen years? Besides, I represented Crosbies in that district later, soon after I went into business."

"Yes, of course. But—I suppose you know the Haymarket pretty well, don't you?"

"Of course I do; both for business and pleasure. Everybody knows the Haymarket."

"Very good. Then tell me the way to St. James's Market."

"There's no such market."

"We have him," said Arnold, with bland triumph. "Literally, he is correct: I believe it's all pulled down now. But it was standing during the war: a small open space with old, low buildings in it, a stone's throw from the back of the tube station. You turned to the right, as you walked down the Haymarket."

"Quite right," confirmed Perrott. "I went there, only once, on the business of an odd magazine that was published in one of those low buildings. But I was talking of Canon's Park, Stoke Newington—"

"I beg your pardon," said Harliss. "I remember now. There is a part in Stoke Newington or near it called Canon's Park. But it isn't a park at all; nothing like a park. That's only a builder's name. It's just a lot of streets. I think there's a Canon's Square, and a Park Crescent, and an Esplanade: there are some decent shops there. But it's all quite ordinary; there's nothing beautiful about it."

"But my cousin said it was an amazing place. Not a bit like the ordinary London parks or anything of the kind he'd seen abroad. You go in through a gateway, and he said it was like finding yourself in another country. Such trees, that must have been brought from the end of the world: there were none like them in England, though one or two reminded him of trees in Kew Gardens; deep hollows with streams running from the rocks; lawns all purple and gold with flowers, and golden lilies too, towering up into the trees, and mixing with the crimson of the flowers that hung from the boughs. And here and there, there were little summer-houses and temples, shining white in the sun, like a view in China, as he put it."

Harliss did not fail with his response, "I tell you there's no such place."

And he added:

"And, anyhow, it all sounds a bit too flowery. But perhaps your cousin was that sort of man: ready to be enthusiastic over a patch of dandeli-ons in a back-garden. A friend of mine once sent me a wire to 'come at once: most important: meet me St. John's Wood Station.' Of course I went, thinking it must be really important; and what he wanted was to show me the garden of a house to let in Grove End Road, which was a blaze of dandelions."

"And a very beautiful sight," said Arnold, with fervour.

"It was a fine sight; but hardly a thing to wire a man about. And I should think that's the secret of all this stuff your cousin told you, Perrott. There used to be one or two big well-kept gardens at Stoke Newington; and I suppose he strolled into one of them by mistake, and then got rather wildly enthusiastic about what he saw."

"It's possible, of course," said Perrott, "but in a general way he wasn't that sort of man. He had an experimental farm, not far from Wells, and bred new kinds of wheat, and improved grasses. I have heard him called stodgy, though I always found him pleasant enough when we met."

"Well, I tell you there's no such place in Stoke Newington or anywhere near it. I ought to know."

"How about St. James's Market?" asked Arnold.

Then, they "left it at that." Indeed, they had felt for some time that they had gone too far away from their known world, and from the friendly tavern fires of the Strand, into the wild no man's land of the north. To Harliss, of course, those regions had once been familiar, common, and uninteresting: he could not revisit them in talk with

any glow of feeling. The other two held them un-
friendly and remote; as if one were to discourse
of Arctic explorations, and lands of everlasting
darkness.

They all returned with relief to their familiar
hunting-grounds, and saw the play in theatres
that had been pulled down for thirty-five years or
more, and had steaks and strong ale afterwards,
in the box by the fire, by the fire that had been
finally raked out soon after the new law courts
were opened.

3

SO, at least, it appeared at the time; but there was something in the tale of this suburban park that remained with Arnold and beset him, and sent him at last to the remote north of the story. For, as he was meditating on this vague attraction, he chanced to light on a shabby brown book on his untidy shelves; a book gathered from a stall in Farringdon Street, where the manuscript of Traherne's *Centuries of Meditations* had been found. So far, Arnold had scarcely glanced at it. It was called, *A London Walk: Meditations in the Streets of the Metropolis*. The author was the Reverend Thomas Hampole, and the book was dated 1853. It consisted for the most part of moral and obvious reflections, such as might be expected from a pious and amiable clergyman of the day. In the middle of the nineteenth century, the relish of moralizing which flourished so in the age of Addison and Pope and Johnson, which made the *Rambler* a popular book, and gave fortunes to the publishers of sermons, had still a great deal of vigour. People liked to be warned of the consequences of their actions, to have lessons in punctuality, to learn about the importance of little things, to hear sermons from stones, and to be taught that there were gloomy reflections to be drawn from almost everything. So then, the Reverend Thomas Hampole stalked the London streets with a moral and monitory glance in his eye: saw Regent Street in its early splendour and thought of the ruins of mighty Rome, preached on the text of solitude in a multitude as he viewed what he called the teeming myriads, and allowed a desolate, half-ruinous house "in Chancery" to suggest thoughts of the happy Christmas parties that had once thoughtlessly revelled behind the crumbling walls and broken windows.

But here and there, Mr. Hampole became less obvious, and perhaps more really profitable. For example, there is a passage—it has already been quoted, I think, by some modern author—which seems curious enough.

Has it ever been your fortune, courteous reader [Mr. Hampole inquired] to rise in the earliest dawning of a summer day, ere yet the radiant beams of the sun have done more than touch with light the domes and spires of the great city? . . . If this has been your lot, have you not observed that magic powers have apparently been at work? The accustomed scene has lost its familiar appearance. The houses which you have passed daily, it may be for years, as you have issued forth on your business or on your pleasure, now seem as if you beheld them for the first time. They have suffered a mysterious change, into something rich and strange. Though they may have been designed with no extraordinary exertion of the art of architecture . . . yet you have been ready to admit that they now "stand in glory, shine like stars, apparelled in a light serene." They have become magical habitations, supernal dwellings, more desirable to the eye than

the fabled pleasure dome of the
Eastern potentate, or the bejewelled
hall built by the Genie for Aladdin
in the Arabian tale.

A good deal in this vein; and then, when one
expected the obvious warning against putting
trust in appearances, both transitory and delu-
sory, there came a very odd passage:

> Some have declared that it lies
> within our own choice to gaze con-
> tinually upon a world of equal or
> even greater wonder and beauty. It
> is said by these that the experiments
> of the alchemists of the Dark Ages
> . . . are, in fact, related, not to the
> transmutation of metals, but to the
> transmutation of the entire Universe
> . . . This method, or art, or science,
> or whatever we choose to call it (sup-
> posing it to exist, or to have ever ex-
> isted), is simply concerned to restore
> the delights of the primal Paradise;
> to enable men, if they will, to inhab-
> it a world of joy and splendour. It is

perhaps possible that there is such an experiment, and that there are some who have made it.

The reader was referred to a note—one of several—at the end of the volume, and Arnold, already a good deal interested by this unexpected vein in the Reverend Thomas, looked it up. And thus it ran:

I am aware that these speculations may strike the reader as both singular and (I may, perhaps, add) chimerical; and, indeed, I may have been somewhat rash and ill-advised in committing them to the printed page. If I have done wrong, I hope for pardon; and, indeed, I am far from advising anyone who may read these lines to engage in the doubtful and difficult experiment which they adumbrate. Still; we are bidden to be seekers of the truth: *veritas contra mundum.*

I am strengthened in my belief that there is at least some foundation for the strange theories at which

I have hinted, by an experience that befell me in the early days of my ministry. Soon after the termination of my first curacy, and after I had been admitted to Priest's Orders, I spent some months in London, living with relations in Kensington. A college friend of mine, whom I will call the Reverend Mr. S——, was, I was aware, a curate in a suburb of the north of London, S.N. I wrote to him, and afterwards called at his lodgings at his invitation. I found S—— in a state of some perturbation. He was threatened, it seemed, with an affection of the lungs and his medical adviser was insistent that he should leave London for awhile, and spend the four months of the winter in the more genial climate of Devonshire. Unless this were done, the doctor declared, the consequences to my friend's health might be of a very serious kind. S—— was very willing to act on this advice, and indeed, anxious to do so; but, on the other hand, he did not wish to resign his curacy, in which, as he said, he was both happy and, he trusted, useful. On hearing this, I at once proffered my services, telling him that if his Vicar approved, I should be happy to do his duty till the end of the ensuing March; or even later, if the physicians considered a longer stay in the south would be advisable. S—— was overjoyed. He took me at once to see the Vicar; the fitting inquiries were made, and I entered on my temporary duties in the course of a fortnight.

It was during this brief ministry in the environs of London, that I became acquainted with a very singular person, whom I shall call Glanville. He was a regular attendant at our services, and, in the course of my duty, I called on him, and expressed my gratification at his evident attachment to the Liturgy of the Church of England. He replied with due politeness, asked me to sit down and partake with him of the soothing cup, and we soon found ourselves engaged in conversation. I discovered early in our association that he was conversant with the reveries of the German Theosophist, Behmen, and the later works of his English disciple, William Law; and it was clear to me that he looked on these labyrinths of mystical theology with a friendly eye. He was a middle-aged man, spare of habit, and of a dark complexion; and his face was illuminated in a very impressive manner, as he discussed the speculations which had evidently occupied his thoughts for many years. Based as these theories were on the doctrines (if we may call them by that name) of Law and Behmen, they struck me as of an extremely fantastic, I would even say fabulous, nature, but I confess that I listened with a considerable degree of interest, while making it evident that as a Minister of the Church of England I was far from giving my free assent to the propositions that were placed before me. They were not, it is true, manifestly and certainly opposed to orthodox belief, but they were assuredly strange, and as such to be received with salutary caution. As an example of the ideas which beset a mind which was ingenious, and I may say, devout, I may mention that Mr. Glanville often dwelt on a consequence, not generally acknowledged, of the Fall of Man. "When man yielded," he would say, "to the mysterious temptation intimated by the figurative language of Holy Writ, the universe, originally fluid and the servant of his spirit, became solid, and crashed down upon him overwhelming him beneath its weight and its dead mass." I requested him to furnish me with more light on this remarkable belief; and I found that in his opinion that which we now regard as stubborn matter was, primally, to use his singular phraseology, the Heavenly Chaos, a soft and ductile substance, which could be moulded by the imagination of uncorrupted man into whatever forms he chose it to assume. "Strange as it may seem," he added, "the wild inventions (as we consider them) of the Arabian Tales give us some notion of the powers of the *homo protoplastus*. The prosperous city becomes a lake, the carpet transports us in an instant of time, or rather without time, from one end of the earth to another, the palace rises at a word from nothingness. Magic, we call all this, while we deride the possibility of any such feats; but this magic of the East is but a confused and fragmentary recollection of operations which were of the first nature of man, and of the fiat which was then entrusted to him."

I listened to this and other similar expositions of Mr. Glanville's extraordinary beliefs with some interest, as I have remarked. I could not but feel that such opinions were in many respects more in accordance with the doctrine I had undertaken to expound than much of the teaching of the philosophers of the day, who seemed to exalt rationalism at the expense of Reason, as that divine faculty was exhibited by Coleridge. Still, when I assented, I made it clear to Glanville that my assent was qualified by my firm adherence to the principles which I had solemnly professed at my ordination.

The months went by in the peaceful performance of the pastoral duties of my office. Early in March, I received a letter from my friend Mr. S——, who informed me that he had greatly benefited by the air of Torquay, and that his medical adviser had assured him that he need no longer hesitate to resume his duties in London. Consequently, S—— proposed to return at once, and, after warmly expressed thanks for my extreme kindness, as he called it, he announced his wish to perform his part in the Church services on the following Sunday. Accordingly, I paid my final visits to those of the parishioners with whom I had more particularly associated, reserving my call on Mr. Glanville for the last day of my residence at S.N. He was sorry,

I think, to hear of my impending departure, and told me that he would always recollect our conversational exchanges with much pleasure.

"I, too, am leaving S.N.," he added. "Early next week I sail for the East, where my stay may be prolonged for a considerable period."

After mutual expressions of polite regret, I rose from my chair, and was about to make my farewells, when I observed that Glanville was gazing at me with a fixed and singular regard.

"One moment," he said, beckoning me to the window, where he was standing. "I want to show you the view. I don't think you have seen it."

The suggestion struck me as peculiar, to say the least of it. I was, of course, familiar with the street in which Glanville resided, as with most of the S.N. streets; and he on his side must have been well aware that no prospect that his window might command could show me anything that I had not seen many times during my four months' stay in the parish. In addition to this, the streets of our London suburbs do not often offer a spectacle to engage the amateur of landscape and the picturesque. I was hesitating, hardly knowing whether to comply with Glanville's request, or to treat it as a piece of pleasantry, when it struck me that it was possible that his first-floor window might afford a distant view of St. Paul's Cathedral; I accordingly stepped to his side, and waited for him to indicate the scene which he, presumably, wished me to admire.

His features still wore the odd expression which I have already remarked.

"Now," said he, "look out and tell me what you see."

Still bewildered, I looked through the window, and saw exactly that which I had expected to see: a row or terrace of neatly designed residences, separated from the highway by a parterre or miniature park, adorned with trees and shrubs. A road, passing to the right of the terrace, gave a view of streets and crescents of more recent construction, and of some degree of elegance. Still, in the whole of the familiar spectacle I saw nothing to warrant any particular attention; and, in a more or less jocular manner, I said as much to Glanville.

By way of reply, he touched me lightly with his finger-tips on the shoulder, and said:

"Look again."

I did so. For a moment, my heart stood still, and I gasped for breath. Before me, in place of the familiar structures, there was disclosed a panorama of unearthly, of astounding beauty. In deep dells, bowered by overhanging trees, there bloomed flowers such as only dreams can show; such deep purples that yet seemed to glow like precious stones with a hidden but ever-present radiance, roses whose hues outshone any that are to be seen in our gardens, tall lilies alive with light, and blossoms that were as beaten gold. I saw well-shaded walks that went down to green hollows bordered with thyme; and here and there the grassy eminence above, and the bubbling well below, were crowned with architecture of fantastic and unaccustomed beauty, which seemed to speak of fairyland itself. I might almost say that my soul was ravished by the spectacle displayed before me. I was possessed by a degree of rapture and delight such as I had never experienced. A sense of beatitude pervaded my whole being; my bliss was such as cannot be expressed by words. I uttered an inarticulate cry of joy and wonder. And then, under the influence of a swift revulsion of terror, which even now I cannot explain, I turned and rushed from the room and from the house, without one word of comment or farewell to the extraordinary man who had done—I knew not what.

In great perturbation and confusion of mind, I made my way into the street. Needless to say, no trace of the phantasmagoria that had been displayed before me remained. The familiar street had resumed its usual aspect, the terrace stood as I had always seen it, and the newer buildings beyond, where I had seen oh! what dells of delight, what blossoms of glory, stood as before in their neat, though unostentatious order. Where I had seen valleys embowered in green leafage, waving gently in the sunshine and the summer breeze, there were now boughs bare and black, scarce showing so much as a single bud. As I have mentioned, the season was early in March, and a black frost which had set in ten days or a fortnight before still constrained the earth and its vegetation.

I walked hurriedly away to my lodgings, which were some distance from the abode of Glanville. I was sincerely glad to think that I was leaving the neighbourhood on the following day. I may say that up to the present moment I have never revisited S.N.

Some months later I encountered my friend Mr. S——, and under cover of asking about the affairs of the parish in which he still ministered, I inquired after Glanville, with whom (I said) I had made acquaintance. It seemed he had fulfilled his intention of leaving the neighbourhood within a few days of my own departure. He had not confided his destination or his plans for the future to anyone in the parish.

"My acquaintance with him," said S——, "was of the slightest, and I do not think that he made any friends in the locality, though he had resided in S.N. for more than five years."

It is now some fifteen years since this most strange experience befell me; and during that period I have heard nothing of Glanville. Whether he is still alive in the distant Orient, or whether he is dead, I am completely ignorant.

4

ARNOLD was generally known as an idle man; and, as he said himself, he hardly knew what the inside of an office was like. But he was laborious in his idleness, and always ready to take any amount of pains, over anything in which he was interested. And he was very much interested in this Canon's Park business. He felt sure that there was a link between Mr. Hampole's odd story—"more than odd," he meditated—and the experience of Perrott's cousin, the wheat-breeder from the west country. He made his way to Stoke Newington, and strolled up and down it, look-ing about him with an inquisitive eye. He found Canon's Park, or what remained of it, without any trouble. It was pretty well as Harliss had described it: a neighbourhood laid out in the twenties or thirties of the last century for City men of comfortable down to tolerable incomes.

Some of these houses remained, and there was an attractive row of old-fashioned shops still surviving. Again, in one place there was the modest cot of late Georgian or early Victorian design, with its trellised porch of faded blue-green paint, its patterned iron balcony, not displeasing, its little garden in the front, and its walled garden at the back; a small coach-house, a small stable. In another, something more exuberant and on a much larger scale: ambitious pilasters and stucco, broad lawns and sweeping drives, towering shrubs, and grass in the back premises. But on all the territory modernism had delivered its assault. The big houses remaining had been made into maisonettes, the small ones were down-at-heel, no longer objects of love; and everywhere there were blocks of flats in wicked red brick, as if Mrs. Todgers had given Mr. Pecksniff her notion of an up-to-date gaol, and he had worked out her design. Opposite Canon's Park, and occupying the site on which Mr. Glanville's house must have stood, was a technical college; next to it a school of economics. Both buildings curdled the blood: in their purpose and in their architecture. They looked as if Mr. H. G. Wells's bad dreams had come true.

In none of this, whether moderately ancient or grossly modern, could Arnold see anything to his purpose. In the period of which Mr. Hampole wrote, Canon's Park may have been tolerably pleasant; it was now becoming intolerably unpleasant. But at its best, there could not have been anything in its aspect to suggest the wonderful vision which the clergyman thought he had seen from Glanville's window. And suburban gardens, however well kept, could not explain the farmer's rhapsodies. Arnold repeated the sacred words of the explanation formula: telepathy, hallucination, hypnotism; but felt very little easier. Hypnotism, for example: that was commonly used to explain the Indian rope trick. There was no such trick, and in any case, hypnotism could not explain that or any other marvel seen by a number of people at once, since hypnotism could only be applied to individuals, and with their full knowledge, consent, and conscious attention. Telepathy might have taken place between Glanville and Hampole; but whence did Perrott's cousin receive the impression that he not only saw a sort of Kubla Khan, or Old Man of the Mountain paradise, but actually walked abroad in it? The S.P.R. had, one might say, discovered telepathy, and had devoted no small part of their energies for the last forty-five years or more to a minute and thoroughgoing investigation of it; but, to the best of his belief, their recorded cases gave no instance of anything so elaborate as this business of Canon's Park. And again; so far as he could remember, the appearances ascribed to a telepathic agency were all personal; visions of people, not of places: there were no telepathic landscapes. And as for hallucination: that did not carry one far. That stated a fact, but offered no explanation of it. Arnold had suffered from liver trouble: he had come down to breakfast one morning and had been vexed to see the air all dancing with black specks. Though he did not smell the nauseous odour of a smoky chimney, he made no doubt at first that the chimney had been smoking, or that the black specks were floating soot. It was some time before he realized that, objectively, there were no black specks, that they were optical illusions, and that he had been hallucinated. And no doubt the parson and the farmer had been hallucinated: but the cause, the motive power, was to seek. Dickens told how, waking one morning, he saw his father sitting by his bedside, and wondered what he was doing there. He addressed the old man, and got no answer, put out his hand to touch him: and there was no such thing. Dickens was hallucinated; but since his father was perfectly well at the time, and in no sort of trouble, the mystery remained insoluble, unaccountable. You had to accept it; but there was no rationale of it. It was a problem that had to be given up.

But Arnold did not like giving problems up. He beat the coverts of Stoke Newington, and dived into pubs of promising aspect, hoping to meet talkative old men, who might remember their fathers' stories and repeat them. He found a few, for though London has always been a place of restless, migratory tribes, and shifting populations; and now more than ever before; yet there still remains in many places, and above all in the remoter northern suburbs, an old fixed element, which can go back in memory sometimes for a hundred, even a hundred and fifty years. So in a venerable tavern—it would have been injurious and misleading to call it a pub—on the borders of Canon's Park he found an ancient circle that gathered nightly for an hour or two in a snug, if dingy, parlour. They drank little and that slowly, and went early home. They were small tradesmen of the neighbourhood, and talked their business and the changes they had seen, the curse of multiple shops, the poor stuff sold in them, and the cutting of prices and profits. Arnold edged into the conversation by degrees, after one or two visits—"Well, sir, I am very much obliged to you, and I won't refuse"—and said that he thought of settling in the neighbourhood: it seemed quiet. "Best wishes, I'm sure. Quiet; well it was, once; but not much of that now in Stoke Newington. All pride and dress and bustle now; and the people that had the money and spent it, they're gone, long ago."

"There were well-to-do people here?" asked Arnold, treading cautiously, feeling his way, inch by inch.

"There were, I assure you. Sound men—warm men, my father used to call them. There was Mr. Tredegar, head of Tredegar's Bank. That was amalgamated with the City and National many years ago: nearer fifty than forty, I suppose. He was a fine gentleman, and grew beautiful pineapples. I remember his sending us one, when my wife was poorly all one summer. You can't buy pineapples like that now."

"You're right, Mr. Reynolds, perfectly right. I have to stock what they call pineapples, but I wouldn't touch them myself. No scent, no flavour. Tough and hard; you can't compare a crabapple with a Cox's pippin."

There was a general assent to this proposition; and Arnold felt that it was slow work.

And even when he got to his point, there was not much gained. He said he had heard that Canon's Park was a quiet part; off the main track.

"Well, there's something in that," said the ancient who had accepted the half-pint. "You don't get very much traffic there, it's true: no trams or buses or motor coaches. But they're pulling it all to pieces; building new blocks of flats every few months. Of course, that might suit your views. Very popular these flats are, no doubt, with many people; most economical, they tell me. But I always liked a house of my own, myself."

"I'll tell you one way a flat is economical," the greengrocer said with a preparatory chuckle. "If you're fond of the wireless, you can save the price and the licence. You'll hear the wireless on the floor above, and the wireless on the floor below, and one or two more besides when they've got their windows open on summer evenings."

"Very true, Mr. Batts, very true. Still, I must say, I'm rather partial to the wireless myself. I like to listen to a cheerful tune, you know, at tea time."

"You don't tell me, Mr. Potter, that you like that horrible jazz, as they call it?"

"Well, Mr. Dickson, I must confess . . ." and so forth, and so forth. It became evident that there were modernists even here: Arnold thought that he heard the term "hot blues" distinctly uttered. He forced another half-pint—"very kind of you; mild this time, if you don't mind"—on his neighbour, who turned out to be Mr. Reynolds, the pharmaceutical chemist, and tried back.

"So you wouldn't recommend Canon's Park as a desirable residence."

"Well, no, sir; not to a gentleman who wants quiet, I should not. You can't have quiet when a place is being pulled down about your ears, as you may say. It certainly was quiet enough in former days. Wouldn't you say so, Mr. Batts?"—breaking in on the musical discussion—"Canon's Park was quiet enough in our young days, wasn't it? It would have suited this gentleman then, I'm sure."

"Perhaps so," said Mr. Batts. "Perhaps so, and perhaps not. There's quiet, and quiet."

And a certain stillness fell upon the little party of old men. They seemed to ruminate, to drink their beer in slower sips.

"There was always something about the place I didn't altogether like," said one of them at last. "But I'm sure I don't know why."

"Wasn't there some tale of a murder there, a long time ago? Or was it a man that killed himself, and was buried at the crossroads by the green, with a stake through his heart?"

"I never heard of that, but I've heard my father say that there was a lot of fever about there formerly."

"I think you're all wide of the mark, gentlemen, if you'll excuse my saying so"—this from an elderly man in a corner, who had said very little hitherto. "I wouldn't say Canon's Park had a bad name, far from it. But there certainly was something about it that many people didn't like; fought shy of, you may say. And it's my belief that it was all on account of the lunatic asylum that used to be there, awhile ago."

"A lunatic asylum was there?" Arnold's particular friend asked. "Well, I think I remember hearing something to that effect in my very young days, now you recall the circumstances. I know we boys used to be very shy of going through Canon's Park after dark. My father used to send me on errands that way now and again, and I always got another boy to come along with me if I could. But I don't remember that we were particularly afraid of the lunatics either. In fact, I hardly know what we were afraid of, now I come to think of it."

"Well, Mr. Reynolds, it's a long time ago; but I do think it was that madhouse put people off Canon's Park in the first place. You know where it was, don't you?"

"I can't say I do."

"Well, it was that big house right in the middle of the park, that had been empty years and years—forty years, I dare say, and going to ruin."

"You mean the place where Empress Mansions are now? Oh, yes, of course. Why they pulled it down more than twenty years ago, and then the land was lying idle all through the war and long after. A dismal-looking old place it was; I remember it well: the ivy growing over the chimney-pots, and the windows smashed, and the 'To Let' boards smothered in creepers. Was that house an asylum in its day?"

"That was the very house, sir. Himalaya House, it was called. In the first place it was built on to an old farmhouse by a rich gentleman from India, and when he died, having no children, his relations sold the property to a doctor. And he turned it into a madhouse. And as I was saying, I think people didn't much like the idea of it. You know, those places weren't so well looked after as they say they are now, and some very unpleasant stories got about; I'm not sure if the doctor didn't get mixed up in a lawsuit over a gentleman, of good family, I believe, who had been shut up in Himalaya House by his relations for years, and as sensible as you or me all the time. And then there was that young fellow that managed to escape: that was a queer business. Though there was no doubt that he was mad enough for anything."

"One of them got away, did he?" Arnold inquired, wishing to break the silence that again fell on the circle.

"That was so. I don't know how he managed it, as they were said to be very strictly kept, but he contrived to climb out or creep out somehow or other, one evening about tea time, and walked as quietly as you please up the road, and took lodgings close by here, in that row of old red-brick houses that stood where the technical college is now. I remember well hearing Mrs. Wilson that kept the lodgings—she lived to be a very old woman—telling my mother that she never saw a nicer-looking, better-spoken young man than this Mr. Valiance—I think he called himself: not his real name, of course. He told her a proper story enough about coming from Norwich, and having to be very quiet on account of his studies and all that. He had his carpetbag in his hand, and said the heavy luggage was coming later, and paid a fortnight in advance, quite regular. Of course, the doctor's men were after him directly and making inquiries in all directions, but Mrs. Wilson never thought for a moment that this quiet young lodger of hers was the missing madman. Not for some time, that is."

Arnold took advantage of a rhetorical pause in the story. He leaned forward to the landlord, who was leaning over the bar, and listening like the rest. Presently orders round were solicited, and each of the circle voted for a small drop of gin, feeling "mild" or even "bitter" to be inadequate to the crisis of such a tale. And then, with courteous expressions, they drank the health of "our friend sitting by our friend Mr. Reynolds." And one of them said:

"So she found out, did she?"

"I believe," the narrator continued, "that it was a week or thereabouts before Mrs. Wilson saw there was something wrong. It was when she was clearing away his tea, he suddenly spoke up, and says:

"'What I like about these apartments of yours, Mrs. Wilson, is the amazing view you have from your windows.'

"Well, you know, that was enough to startle her. We all of us know what there was to see from the windows of Rodman's Row: Fothergill Terrace, and Chatham Street, and Canon's Park: very nice properties, no doubt, all of them, but nothing to write home about, as the young people say. So Mrs. Wilson didn't know how to take it quite, and thought it might be a joke. She put down the tea-tray, and looked the lodger straight in the face.

"'What is it, sir, you particularly admire, if I might ask?'

"'What do I admire?' said he. 'Everything.' And then, it seems, he began to talk the most outrageous nonsense about golden and silver and purple flowers, and the bubbling well, and the walk that went under the trees right into the wood, and the fairy house on the hill; and I don't know what. He wanted Mrs. Wilson to come to the window and look at it all. She was frightened, and took up her tray, and got out of the room as quick as she could; and I don't wonder at it. And that night, when she was going up to bed, she passed her lodger's door, and heard him talking out loud, and she stopped to listen. Mind you, I don't think you can blame the woman for listening. I dare say she wanted to know who and what she had got in her house. At first she couldn't make out what he was saying. He was jabbering in what sounded like a foreign language; and then he cried out in plain English as if he were talking to a young lady, and making use of very affectionate expressions.

"That was too much for Mrs. Wilson, and she went off to bed with her heart in her boots, and hardly got to sleep all through the night. The next morning the gentleman seemed quiet enough, but Mrs. Wilson knew he wasn't to be trusted, and directly after breakfast she went round to the neighbours, and began to ask questions. Then, of course, it came out who her lodger must be, and she sent word round to Himalaya House. And the doctor's men took the young fellow back. And, bless my soul, gentlemen; it's close on ten o'clock."

The meeting broke up in a kind of cordial bustle. The old man who had told the story of the escaped lunatic had remarked, it appeared, the very close attention that Arnold had given to the tale. He was evidently gratified. He shook Arnold warmly by the hand, remarking: "So you see, sir, the grounds I have for my opinion that it was that madhouse that gave Canon's Park rather a bad name in our neighbourhood."

And Arnold, revolving many things, set out on the way back to London. Much seemed heavily obscure, but he wondered whether Mrs. Wilson's lodger was a madman at all; any madder than Mr. Hampole, or the farmer from Somerset or Charles Dickens, when he saw the appearance of his father by his bed.

5

ARNOLD told the story of his researches and perplexities at the next meeting of the three old friends in the quiet court leading into the inn. The scene had changed into a night in June, with the trees in the inn garden fluttering in a cool breeze, that wafted a vague odour of hayfields far away into the very heart of London. The liquor in the brown jar smelt of Gascon vineyards and herb-gardens, and ice had been laid about it, but not for too long a time.

Harliss's word all through Arnold's tale was:

"I know every inch of that neighbourhood, and I told you there was no such place."

Perrott was judicial. He allowed that the history was a remarkable one: "You have three witnesses," Arnold had pointed out.

"Yes," said Perrott, "but have you allowed for the marvellous operation of the law of coincidences? There's a case, trivial enough, perhaps you may think, that made a deep impression on me when I read it, a few years ago. Forty years before, a man had bought a watch in Singapore—or Hong Kong, perhaps. The watch went wrong, and he took it to a shop in Holborn to be seen to. The man who took it from him over the counter was the man who had sold him the watch in the East all those years before. You can never put coincidence out of court, and dismiss it as an impossible solution. Its possibilities are infinite."

Then Arnold told the last broken, imperfect chapter of the story.

"After that night at the King of Jamaica," he began, "I went home and thought it all over. There seemed no more to be done. Still, I felt as if I would like to have another look at this singular park, and I went up there one dark afternoon. And then and there I came upon the young man who had lost his way, and had lost—as he said— the one who lived in the white house on the hill. And I am not going to tell you about her, or her house, or her enchanted gardens. But I am sure that the young man was lost also—and for ever."

And after a pause, he added:

"I believe that there is a perichoresis, an inter-penetration. It is possible, indeed, that we three are now sitting among desolate rocks, by bitter streams . . . And with what companions?"

A PARTIAL LIST OF SNUGGLY BOOKS